JUNO VALENTINE
AND THE FANTASTIC FASHION ADVENTURE

WRITTEN BY
EVA CHEN

ILLUSTRATED BY
DEREK DESIERTO

FEIWEL AND FRIENDS · NEW YORK

A FEIWEL AND FRIENDS BOOK
An imprint of Macmillan Publishing Group, LLC
120 Broadway, New York, NY 10271

Our books may be purchased in bulk for promotional, educational, or business use.
Please contact your local bookseller or the Macmillan Corporate and Premium Sales Department
at (800) 221-7945 ext. 5442 or by email at MacmillanSpecialMarkets@macmillan.com.

Library of Congress Control Number: 2019931339
ISBN 978-1-250-29730-3 (hardcover) / ISBN 978-1-250-26308-7 (ebook)

Book design by Carol Ly
Feiwel and Friends logo designed by Filomena Tuosto
First edition, 2019

1 3 5 7 9 10 8 6 4 2

mackids.com

FOR REN AND TAO,

MAY YOU ALWAYS MARCH TO
THE BEAT OF YOUR OWN DRUM.

It was just another Monday morning and, to the surprise of the entire Valentine family, Juno was exactly on time for school.

MOM, I'M READY! LET'S GO TO SCHOOL!

Miss Dahlia always started the school day with announcements, and today she had an especially important one.

"Tomorrow is school picture day . . . Wear something that makes you feel magical."

After school, Juno and her friends pondered the possibilities.

Trixie had a grand plan: "I know *exactly* what I'll wear tomorrow . . . I'm going to be a gloriously glacial ice princess."

Shiona too: "F-f-fashion with a capital F!"

And Wells was born ready: "Come on, *Vogue*."

"Juno, what are *you* going to wear?!"

That night, Juno racked her brain.

It was a fashion conundrum!

Her mom would want her to wear her most fabulous florals.

Her dad would want her to wear her rainbow ruffles.

Trixie, Shiona, and Wells would want her to wear anything other than her same old look.

Her brother Finn . . .

Wait . . . where on earth was Finn going?

Juno followed Finn
into her closet and . . .

Oh no, not again!

Juno was back in the magical hall of
shoes, and her brother was about to make a
major mess.

"Finn Valentine! Do *not* touch those shoes!"

As usual, Finn did not listen to his big sister.

Juno watched as her brother slipped on a
pair of swashbuckling boots and . . .

"Ahoy, matey!"

"You look like a girl who's about to go on a grand adventure—take my hat," said pirate Grace O'Malley. "It'll give you gumption."

"And here's a perfect pair of pants I picked up in Rome," said Audrey Hepburn as she waltzed by. "Don't forget to dance, Juno . . . it makes everything infinitely more fun! Give it a whirl."

Juno had a pirate hat. Juno had perfect pants. But Juno
needed a plan to catch her brother.

"I can draft something for you," offered Maya Lin.

"With conviction and proper planning, anything's possible."

"The plan says head west!" bellowed Annie Oakley.

"Nice bandanna, by the way. But it needs a little fringe! Pow!

Now it's perfect. You'll look great in your school picture."

Maya's map was a miracle! It led
Juno to a plethora of awesome women
who all wanted to help.
Juno got . . .

Shoulder pads from
Grace Jones: "They'll
make you feel fierce!"

A shimmering cape from Joan of Arc:
"Don't be afraid, Juno! You were born to do this."

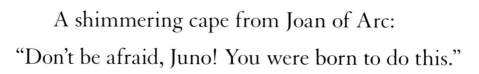

A banana skirt from Josephine Baker:
"This chase is B-A-N-A-N-A-S!"

Marie Antoinette was, to be honest,
not much help at all.

"I really don't do chases. But I do enjoy cake.
Would you like a bonbon?"

No matter how fast Juno ran, her rapscallion brother was always one step ahead.

"Finn is way too fast. I'll never catch him," sighed Juno. "I can't do this!"

Juno felt a comforting hand on her shoulder. "Yes, you can, Juno," said Michelle Obama. "Here, take my boots. They're my most marvelous possession—I'm extra confident in them. Maybe they'll work some magic for you too."

Juno made the final sprint with a spring in her step. When she turned the corner she found . . .

a balance beam?

According to Maya's plan, the fastest way to catch
Finn would be to cartwheel and somersault across the beam!
But gymnastics had never been easy for Juno.

"Sometimes," said Simone Biles as she placed a gold medal around Juno's neck, "you just have to take a leap of faith and trust yourself. You know who you are. You can do it."

Juno took a deep breath, made a great big LEAP, and . . .

She caught Finn!

It'd been the zaniest of nights, but Juno and Finn were finally home.

And—yikes!—it was time to leave for school!

JUNO VALENTINE

MOST LIKELY TO BE . . .
HERSELF AND NO ONE ELSE.

MISS DAHLIA'S
SECOND GRADERS

JUNO'S GUIDE TO GROUNDBREAKING WOMEN

GRACE O'MALLEY
Always be yourself! This utterly fearless Irish pirate queen defied traditions and gender norms in the 16th century to live a remarkable life on both land and sea.

AUDREY HEPBURN
Elegance personified, this award-winning actor and dancer was also a humanitarian who devoted herself to causes such as UNICEF. What do *you* do to make a difference?

MAYA LIN
Age is just a number: this American architect and artist achieved international recognition at just 21 years old when her design was selected for the Vietnam Veterans Memorial in Washington, DC.

ANNIE OAKLEY
This spirited American sharpshooter bested many a man in the 1800s to become internationally recognized (even by the Queen of England).

GRACE JONES
Dress for success: this model, actor, and artist helped inspire the neo-cubist art movement with her iconic fashion sense and androgynous style.

JOAN OF ARC
When told she couldn't fight because she was a girl, Joan cropped her hair and dressed in boys' clothes. She led the French army to victory in a critical battle in 1429 and was later recognized as a saint.

JOSEPHINE BAKER
More than meets the eye: Baker wasn't just a world-renowned dancer—she was also a World War II spy, an activist, and an outspoken critic against segregation and discrimination.

MARIE ANTOINETTE
Marie Antoinette became the French queen at 19 years old and lived a life of excess in the 18th century.

MICHELLE OBAMA
Dream big (but work hard too): Obama is a lawyer, writer, advocate, and the first-ever African American First Lady of the United States.

SIMONE BILES
Considered by many (including this author!) to be the best gymnast ever, Biles holds the record for most world titles by a gymnast, male or female.